Jay Griffiths

First published 2007
this first edition limited to three thousand copies
© Jay Griffiths 2007

Published in the UK by Wooden Books Ltd.
8a Market Place, Glastonbury, Somerset

British Library Cataloguing in Publication Data
Griffiths, J.

Anarchipelago

ISBN 978-1904263-23-4

Hare illustration by Peter Fox

100% recycled waste papers throughout.
No trees were harmed to make this book.

Printed and bound in Wiltshire, UK
by The Cromwell Press, Trowbridge.
Special recycled papers from Paperback.

WOODEN
BOOKS

AN aRcHi pELaGO

—

Jay Griffiths

Dedicated to Britain's road protesters

If you drive along the A34 past Newbury this afternoon or tomorrow night, summer or winter, you will, whether you know it or not, be driving over a spirited land. Under the tarmac of the fast lane is a pixie spirit of glee. Under the middle lane, a robust spirit of courage. Under the slow lane, as deep and certain as earth, an older spirit of honour. And along every inch where the hard shoulder meets the grass and thistles, the two most irrepressible spirits of all: love and life. For love of life, for green, green life, a piece of theatre was played here in the mid-nineties, when hundreds of people camped in treehouses and benders to try to stop the road being built through a landscape of surpassing beauty.

Some of the players were tangly pissheads and some were darlings of innocence. Some invented an idiosyncratic architecture out of trash and some flew their words like kites from the treetops. Some fought funny, some fought angry, some fought stoned. They fought and failed to stop this particular road being built, but they succeeded in ambushing the imagination of a nation, and did so with flair and fury and fire.

Some came and blew a thoughtful breath to the flame. A few burned out and their part in this play left them charred. More, though, came and found their souls lit from this strange fire. A difficult fire, a fantasmagoric fire, a fire fit for a phoenix. This is written for them all. Crucially, it was also written by them all – it is fiction but it is also a truth, a record of my respect for all the players who put their liveliness on the line and who stepped then across the walkways between trees by starlight, and who step again now across these pages. "I found the poems in the fields and only wrote them down," said John Clare, England's peasant poet. Anarchipelago is a kind of "found fiction", a story I heard in the mud and treehouses in that extraordinary time.

ANARCHIPELAGO

BOILING hot day, McTypical McSuburb, McTypical McSunday. I'm watching the neighbours, all the neighbours, going into their gardens to mow the litter.

"Roddy." (Mum.)

"Roddy?" (Mum.)

"RODDY."

"Mum?"

"Go and put a sunshade over the tree. Its leaves are getting sunburned."

Voice like baking powder. I like her, but voice like baking powder.

"Roddy." (Dad.)

"Roddy?" (Dad.)

"RODDY."

(I wish I could kick this habit. I can't. It's my age.) "Dad?"

"Where's the paint?"

Pause. So soon. Between the missing pot and the pavement arrival. Between the two is Dad. Leaps to conclusions, he knows where he is with a conclusion, a vegetable solution; he can get a good thud off of a conclusion like a parsnip on wood.

"Look at what he's done." Dad to Mum. She looks from the kitchen window. I look from the bedroom window. I'm lost in admiration. Come-swimming admiration, wash-in-me admiration, drink-me admiration. Paint pert to the road. White cheeky to the black. Each rectangle a sweet statement, cross over, pedestrian, old ladies and zimmers shall walk free, and the meek need not cower in the disabled parking spaces. You don't have to be religious to know a beatitude in motion. It's a humble art, but valuable, DIY zebra crossings. Take my advice, though, don't do it outside your own house and don't do it with your Dad's paint.

"His degree's wasted on him."

This is the bell. My time is up.

"Give him a chance."

It isn't a chance I want. It's Freedom.

*

One day fair drizzles into another day sunny. Wimbly. Tidy as a crematorium in Wimbly. Nature beige in tooth and claw in Wimbly. Nothing left to jump. No bad luck, no, but no good luck either. No nasty loose roof slates to chip a corner off your IQ, no, but no fivers down the settee, either. No visible sewage, no, but no splendour either. No bitten-twice feuds, no, but no flashflood friendships either.

Same small problems, same smoothly solutions, dilute you to

a simple dissolution. Salty vigour is soothed to tasteless paste in Wimbly, life's cliffs are fenced off for your own protection, burning noons of excess are washed in tepid detergents. Wipe-clean conversations and formica remarks, in Wimbly. Suburbia uses only vowels, no consonants. Vowels are plastic and don't collect dust. Consonants, shoddy, silky or grainy, have difficult corners and rough surfaces.

Out on the bromide lawn, or in on the convenience couch, through the torpor of non-events, ease your, pamper your, relax your, soothe your softened greed, from your sebaceous waking to your adipose repose.

YA BASTARDOS! VIVA LA FUCK-THIS-FOR-A-LIFADISTAS.

I daydream. When Wimbly-staines are mildly inconvenient, simply banish unsightly rows of houses with the amazing duzzitduzzit device, easy to use, portable, suitable for all types of siburbin streets. With the modern convenient simper-sniper, NoWetWonderCream cleanses away suburb after suburb, simply applicate the Duzzit device with NoWetWonderCream, simply point the unit and simply press the button. Ideal for you to operate from the bathroom or bedroom, it comes with a bargain price aromatherapy fragrance facility; simply clip it on, handy for those difficult cornershop smells. Modern technology means you can simply wipe-clean the perimeters of a town, large or small. And all without messy wetting.

I repair to my allotment and tend the Giant Hogweed. Giant Hogweed. There's a plant. More undisciplined than curly kale, more splendid than Chaucer at Speakers' Corner, hungrier than the belly of jealousy, Giant Hogweed (-ignore it at your peril, turn your back and it'll bite your arse-) Giant Hogweed is the uncarpeted chuckle of nature in the raw.

Three seedlings are ready but I need to wait for night. I go home and put my armchair out in the middle of the road until I hear the squeak of air through lips pursed with the creed of Indignatious, the sound of Mrs and Mr Simon Simons, talking at my dad, speaking right ahead of their faces in parallel whines.

"We're up fed with Roderick, aren't we, dear, we're out put with Roderick, aren't we dear, he hums, doesn't he dear, more than is normal, he's up all night and he sleeps all day, he visits skips, he leaves marks on the pavement, he obstructs traffic from the comfort of his blinking armchair and worst of all we think he gets a laugh at our expense, don't we dear?"

Dad, with a face like stone cladding: "He's our son. Naff off."

He's where I get it from, though lobsters would pass their driving tests before either of us would admit it. Mrs Simon Simons has to go home and support her sagging jaw with a Chin Gym ("simply hold the mouthpiece between your teeth for fifteen minutes daily") - but she catches me later on the pavement and goes bombast and florid at me.

Don't give that anger too warm a welcome, Mrs Simons. Pricey is the cost of anger, these days, Mrs Simons, increasing the risk of heart disease. No NHS to speak of, to be irritated is to risk having to up your private health insurance premiums. Vexation never came cheap, but I am particularly expensive. I don't say any of this, but I give her a grin like spiny restharrow. (Dried.)

*

Today, more than usual, my freedom hurts me; from the inside. My freedom of movement isn't allowed to roam the earth, for there is only concrete, so it rubs inside my boots, freedom digging into my feet at the instep. My freedom of speech is silenced by the limits of what can be heard in Wimbly, and this freedom aches my throat tacit. My breath chokes on Wimbly's traffic congestion, so my free air suffocates my lungs. My body is charged full of freedoms, it knows the horizons of its inheritance, but there is nowhere for these freedoms to go except into the ethereal realm, freedom-as-hallucination, eleutheria.

Night. Night is the only time when there's enough space for me in Wimbly. Sunny daylight shrink wraps the suburbs but makes me swollen, bruising my cheek on ceilings, my eyelashes catch on Venetian blinds, I stub my toe on a bungalow or two. But night comes vaster than the all of things, wider than width itself and deeper than the soul of size.

Now is there night. Now is there room for me. I dig in the mud with my fingers around the seedlings. And mud is a sensible thing. Mud and me humour the seedlings into newspaper. No one in Wimbly knows that cultivating Giant Hogweed to plant wild is illegal. No one except me and G.H. Sirself.

Number 14 has a twittering sprinkle of carnations in the garden. Number 14 thinks Nature should be tucked like tupperware between the garage and Gardeners' Questiontime. Number 14 thinks Radix Malorum Ground Elder Est. They do not know what Giant Hogweed can do.

There is something else. Number 14 is the home of Mr McWhinney. Mr McWhinney does his gardening with a gas-powered weed wand, which scorches them to death, to be simply swept away. But worse than weeds, Mr McWhinney hates filth. Mud does not like him, earth keeps its distance and soil is shy. And Mr McWhinney is really exercised by rumours of human dirt, bunches of nogood boyos, New Age Lazy Bastards, road protesters and travellers, who do not like living in houses, but want to live outdoors, who relish not stayputtishness, who seek the open road. Even Wimbly has spawned a few of these tadpoles. Mr McWhinney McWhines to the local Wimbly newspaper and they print what he writes, for he is an businessman. "They are absolutely primitive, and they look like ancient Britons," he says, and does not know how they take that as a compliment.

Mr McWhinney has a dog, which would like to bark at me. But Mr McWhinney also has a barkbuster for his dog. It scowls at me now, but it won't bark, because every time it does, it gets an electric shock, "mild static correction," off of its collar.

Night is with me. Here, at Number 14, I get my green spraypaint to the rub of his house wall. The first graffiti is up. I woz 'ere. "*Hic eram ego*" is what I spray. There's nothing to beat

Latin for scaring the neighbours; they start to think the enemy is within. People who write graffiti go to state schools; state schools don't teach Latin. Q.E.D. (Quite Easily Done.)

Peaty earth, at Number 14. Bought in. Wimbly's tends to the clay by rights. Smells cosmetic here, like they scent it with peat extract, essence of Eire. This peat is John Lewis, ground floor, perfume counter, too much makeup, peat. Peat; New Labour. Mud; Old Labour.

Dad's right. My degree's wasted on me, and I on it. He said as much to my tutor. Dad gave him the look, one part admiration, two parts pity that till then he'd reserved for my girlfriends. (Gina, the last, went to step classes and left me for her greed therapist. I wasn't sorry. Dad devasted.) "Politics and art and do you ever think he'll get a job?"

"He's growing up in a democracy," said the testy tutor, "he can choose."

Child of Thatcher that I am, in so far as I grew up in Wimbly, blue to the third rinse, I grew up in a democracy. In so far as I grew up in Britain, I did not. I spare them this nice paradox.

Rub a little hole in the earth, seeing with my hands, dim to the thumbs, hear the odd hum of earthcrumb on earthcrumb. In go the seedlings at Number 14. My guerrilla gardening is a success.

Lights snap on. Leccy upstairs and down. Leccy light outside. Surveillance camera flashes. Leg it.

*

"Roddy." (Mum.)

"RODDY," (Dad.)

"RODERICK." (Mr McWhinney, Mum and Dad.)

Fuck.

*

I read about the Dongas, once, in the newspaper. Amazing piece, journalism fit to stop you in your porridge. Apart from being road protesters, the thing that really impressed me was their grubbiness. Came clean off the page at you. One look and there they were, mud after my own heart, partners in grime. But more. They sat in the earth to stop a road being built through beauty. Wept like rain at the grief of nature. Justice in their eyes like the original loam.

I stuck the piece in the allotment shed and never forgot it. When you want to run, Roddy, run with them. Ideas germinate like that, dark in your mind's soil for months. Suddenly a combination happens of wet and warmth, and they up pop, peagreen and poddy, idea become action, on the green split of now.

I pack a cheap black plastic holdall, a sadly sadly sorry little thing, and I find me a train.

Woman opposite, (blue eyes, pink rims; good shoes, bad marriage,) tries to talk to me. I fold her gambits under the seat and wish the shush of her, no offence. Would rather trains divided into speaking or non-speaking. Pretend to sleep.

The inside of my head is far too light to sleep. Grapes of freedom explode like an illegal summer street party. Arriving at Newbury has my nerves shrilling like a whenny pistle fought over by three-year-olds. I leave my sad-bag on the train by mistake.

*

It is long after midnight, and I look for a camp, any camp, in the dark. All along the proposed route of the Newbury bypass are various camps, some on the ground, some in the trees, some with four people living in them, some with forty. Knee deep in nature and night, hedges tangle me with their hedgey grievance. Paths start out strong, but end split in rancorous splinters, squandering their original ambition like leftie political groups, lost in squabble, sparring into the ground.

Ditch-dodging exhausts me. The idea of ditch-dwelling, though, at four a.m. has a turvy hospitality and I stop, rootwad grumbling at my ankles. Quiet as felt, dumb quiet, mole quiet, but.

"Ferk erf ye cunt ye and find yer own ferking ditch. Perlease."

It is true. Of all the ditches in all the leafy environs of Newbury, I have found probably the only one already inhabited.

I go on. Frankly, now, I hate nature, and I wish there was

a great big, flat, smooth, simple, grey ROAD to easypeesy me along. At dawn, and only at dawn, I stumble on a camp. There are banners and slogans in the trees, wood carvings and wickermen in the forest clearings. There are a few treehouses and several benders on the ground; hazel twigs and willow bent over and covered with tarpaulin for shelter. There is a kitchen bender with a makeshift sink, a sophisticated recycling system and too many cabbages, and nearby is a yellow coach with three wheels and a huge sunflower growing through the roof. It has been raining, and the paths are well trod between the shit pit and the benders, the teepees and the treehouses and the firepit. The whole place is an ode to mud.

I lift the skirts of a few shacky benders. One heavy tarpaulin drapes an area stuffed with people, rugs, blankets and tat. I crawl in, cold, damp, sick of everything, burrowing into the middle of Everybody, warm wool and fuggy Everybody, sweaty biscuity Everybody, smoky, cidery, buttery Everybody.

Sleep.

Two hours later, a voice: "In the night, someone reared up, dropped his sleeping bag and pissed like a horse right here where I'm stood now. So, no bare feet, it's wetter than it should be."

I get up and find a grubby mug and a kettle with half an inch of warm water. I stir some gravy granules into it by mistake and then Lisa, so-called Lisa-the-Lift makes me a splitter; real coffee, real milk, hot water, all in a mug with clean insides. Lisa-the-Lift, with a don't-expect-but-trying look about her, a nevertheless-someone's-got-to strain in her vowel sounds, wants to show me the route, for Lisa-the-Lift, reliably sober, has a car. We walk it.

Dark wood. Enchanter's nightshade, small but tenacious, is growing like a Lets scheme in the middle of fern-suburbs. Banks of wild garlic grow in sticky clumps, thickly sufficient unto itself, like an inner-city Cypriot community. Cow parsley everywhere, the docile classes, the bank holiday classes, flatsummer and Whitsun caravans on stabilisers, never-voted-anything-but. Then buttercups, heart in the right place, geography in the wrong, buttercups, sweetsixteen, still humming Free-ey Nel-Sonman-Dalai, imprisoned leader of Tibet, long after his release, buttercups in tweety cheesecloth dresses kissing up daisies. Just past adolescence myself, how I can scorn it.

The bypass route is a splash painting of all my Englands, crossing all kinds of countryside from Rack Marsh, where pale water meets paler sky, and flat water, flatter sky. Reeds in silence. At Kennet canal, there are bricky bridges, muddy towpaths, ivy gates, one with a felt tip sign in wonky little letters saying "Please shut the gate," and it won't. A woman passes, walking her dogs, chest like a cupboard, galoshes, headscarf and stance. Snelsmore Common is woody, pathy and oaky. At Rickety Bridge, streams run to the watermeadows. Donnington Castle is stone of my England. Two civil war battles were fought here, and the third is just now beginning. We return.

Some cerulean evening. A few people from the Donga tribe arrive at sunset. Oxen, horses, handcarts, dreadlocks, fires, carved wooden spoons, the open road, more sky, more sky, more sky. No tupperware, and I can breathe for the first time in my life. Did I believe in pixies and were gypsies a thing of the past? I know I have never thought it possible.

It is solidly three days before I am over the shock, though it may be that the mushrooms have an apology to make. Someone shows me a Hopi dream catcher, the feather and web which tangle bad dreams and let good ones through. Or the other way round. I sleep in someone's bender, dizzy with joy, and a little photocopy of teepee etiquette hangs over the door. What time is it? I ask before I pass out. Some dryad with a lovely tilt on him says Time is a Swiss invention used to sell watches, and a girl with iris eyes swims naked past me. My capacity for happiness is limitless, my happacity full for the puff like a bagpipe for the song.

It can't last, and it doesn't. When I wake I have the Hopi dream-catcher caught in my flies. I've been bitten by mosquitoes, my head hurts and a minor eye infection plays havoc with my sex-appeal. There are leaflets around the bender, copies of Squall, and Schnews, RoadAlert pamphlets. Reading makes my stomach give in and I lurch out of the bender to go and throw up behind a Turkish yurt.

Ruby-the-delightful, the girl with iris eyes, says, "You'll be fine when I've got a healing bender sorted." Nature heals the Dongas, gentle, soothing and none so honeyed. My nature has nasty little ticks and gives you itchy rashes. They use dock leaves. I want Dettol. Ruby offers me some herb tea, free produce of nature, tea of surpassing innocence. I want Nescafé, baby-killers all, and Anadin Extra, only with a trademark.

It dawns. It's not really part of Donga philosophy to be a hypochondriac. I would never make a good Donga, but the fact of it makes me sad, so that I can't get warm for hours. I doze. I dream of bathroom cabinets filled with plastic capsules of instant symptom-relief.

"You have to cure the cause. It's more holistic."

"Fuck holism, my head hurts."

Ruby starts to go. She's going to leave me on my horrible tod. I don't blame her. Nor would you, just now, sweet unmetyet you.

"Wait," I wail. She waits. I'm going to cry. I don't fit, and I've never wanted to fit so badly. I don't belong. A shattering, heartbreaking, simileless state. I jolt it out to her: "I don't fit in."

"You can learn." Soft. Nice. She's nice. They're all nice. I'm not. No one's ever said I'm nice. Really. What I don't say is I don't know if I want to learn. I don't even know if I want to stay. But then I think of Wimbly seeping all across this country of mine, my England. Soil. Rain. Treescape. I think of my government. Corruption. Cruelty. The CJA. I love my country and I hate my state. But I'm still undecided. Then I think of Ruby, and that settles it. I'm staying for the nonce, however long a nonce is.

I go skipping. The skip, I am learning, is to be source of all my wants except Ruby, grass and polyprop. The skip, if you're poor, is a fickle loss-adjustor. Today, you find unsuspected gifts, but tomorrow, you may find nothing, and poverty hangs precarious between them. Today, I find the wood for a treehouse platform with beginner's luck.

I start looking around for a good tree to build a treehouse in.

There is something of the sempiternal about an oak. Oak scorns to jump with man's fashions, it shrugs off the mere. The original I AM was oak and it disdains the proof of it. Robustus ego et Rex sum and doesn't reckon much to man. Us; bindweed and tinsel. Oak; pith, wood and integrity to the tug of things. (Nul points for a sense of humour, though, in an oak.)

Think like a tree. Feel where the weight will sit best, lash the wood, don't nail it. I make a hammock for myself in the branches, and I lie in it, wrapped up like a toffee. A week after I arrived, I sleep the first of many nights up my tree, and when I wake the birds are singing, below me. I spend several days building the platform and walls. I start getting used to long perspectives, living at that height, and discover a great respect for gravity. My senses are quickened to changes of weather and season, and I feel enlivened in the animal department of myself. Trees are living things to live in, houses are not alive. It becomes a relationship. I wouldn't go so far as to call it my commonlaw tree, but you live close to it, and you feel its moods, you get its bark on your clothes, its moss under your fingernails and you wear its leaves in your hair. You hug your tree - of course you do - and it holds you all night.

For me, I am satisfying my nesting instinct; until I was thirteen I thought I should have been a bird. They symbolize freedom as much to me as ever they did to medieval wattlers and daubers. Freedom. Here, if anywhere, I might find the freedom I seek, the freedom of air and sap and water and night.

*

There is a bird called the familiar chat. It doesn't live in Newbury and I wish it did. Stephen-the-Grievance does. I wish he didn't. He wastes two hours (of my time and clearly not his,) moaning in my tree, and lightening his dirge with lines from the dead parrot sketch. To escape him, I go into town and while I'm there, I blag money from the protest office funds for a piece of tarpaulin to roof the top of my treehouse. It takes most of the day; ten minutes for getting the OK from OK Simon, and four and a half hours chilling out in the Valhalla smokeasy, the only office space in the south of England where people object to your not smoking dope.

The DIY-cum-builders-merchants have been told by the council and the police that they are not allowed to sell goods to protesters. I wander round the pity of the place, this wonderland of tackle and fitting. The politics of the DIY shop are beautiful; the politics of possibility and of self-respect, the manifesto of make it yourself, build your own vision. The DIY shop appeals to the self-determining republican in everyone. Gerrymandering is impotent before a toolkit, Lady Porter gets nailed in the timber yard. Woodglue is the undaunted soul of courage, can-do resistance is the hammer-blow for independence; liberty, egality and fraternity is the spanner, the axe and the jemmy. With Cavour on the screwdriver and Garibaldi on the saw, the chords of the risorgimento are restruck anew.

"Can I buy some tarp?"

"Nope," says the assistant.

I ask to see the manager.

"No," he can't wait to tell me. "No, HAA. We'd be aiding and abetting. The police have asked us not to."

Body in an M and S suit, mind in Stanley Matthews shorts, his ideas far too big for his biglittle mind. Behold the man-manager, biglittle panjandrum. Here he is, ecce homo, the backbone of England. Refusing to sell me my tarp is the closest he'll ever get to Power. He swells with pleasure, biglittle inglinder, eyes wet with Cromwell, the Blitz, the Falklands and Thatcher. He loves his nation. I want my tarp to protect my oak, my corner of England. I love my land. England, his England, comes to him in dreams. England, my England, is being shrunk in the wash.

"OK," I say, suddenly compliant. He's more on guard than ever, his sus-finger trembly on the bayonet, don't-panic-Mr-Mainwaring in his lower lip.

"Sell me a Union Jack, then."

It causes him real pain. Am I friend now or foe? Perplexity harrows him, he is a man who wants to know where he stands, and who he is standing on.

"Please."

He goes to the stockroom and is back within seconds. My

beautiful Union Jack. £14.99. Bankruptcy, but I want it. I pay with a twenty quid note. He checks it elaborately.

"Keep the change," I say, and bolt for it.

He's probably seen the tarp stuffed up my coat. I don't care; I paid for it. What I haven't paid for is the spanner in one boot, the saw blade up my sleeve and the axe down my pants. (Don't put axes down your pants, it's not worth the anxiety, and what anxiety wants it steals from your sperm count.)

I leave, bumping into the splendour that is King Arthur in the car park. Arthur Uther Pendragon, reincarnation of your once and future, is a fully paid-up member of the awkward brigade, according to the Newbury rag, or shrewd litigant fighting the CJA in the courts of justice, depending on your point of view. Just now though, he is sweaty with the hair shirt, and, has got Excalibur caught up in the steering-lock of Lisa-the-Lift's car. "I'm jes on me way to the bank then I'm erf ter fertify Camelert." I know that voice. We once nearly shared a ditch.

*

Summer changes to autumn, and mists smudge the canal. There's an enviable grace in the turn of seasons, a regalism that almost brings out the monarchist in me. Arthur would be proud. But it's also at the pause between seasons, such as this, that nature has a habit of coming over all symbolic at me. Nature is stuffed full of abstract nouns; hope is skylarks. Vandalism is squirrels. Freedom is everything. My need for freedom - freedom, take it or steal it - is, I realise now, being met here. I had thought that freedom was the gift of democracy, from free elections to free associations. Not necessarily so. How humbled now and how late I know that the freedom I fled for is not in anyone's gift, but nature's. I feel it inside me, for living here has brought down the fences, has repealed the enclosures between my inner landscapes and the woodlands outside me. I am nature, and it is me. Inside me is all outdoors, open tundra in my eyes, veld across my chest, pampas in my armpits, steppes at my elbows and knees, savanna across my stomach, moorland and cliffs in my head.

While these thoughts hang clear and colourful across my mind like prayer flags across a Tibetan mountain pass, I call Ruby-the-delightful quick to my tree. Ruby, not enough space on her face for both herself and her smile - let alone mine - is my confidante and comes with the cider. But when I try to explain, I get no further than my bollocks-the-bushveld-type-thing and I go quiet, as you would. A few tipplish licks of Merrydown persuade me to save my thoughts until I find you to tell, whenever the late youever. Who are not yet.

Ruby's eyes up close, though, see the irises like cross-sections through tree trunks, give me courage to start again, but all I can say is "I love this place, Rube." (Ruby likes love.) And what I can't say is "and I hate its enemies." (For Ruby doesn't like hate. It's the only thing I hate about her.) So I say again, "I love this place," and what I mean is this: I have never felt an emotion quite like this, this impassioned altruism, needing both love and hate, love running savage to protect what it loves. Love like a waterfall with rocks of fury behind it.

"Whatever it takes, Ruby, whatever it takes." It comes out sounding like a vow, and I don't know why. It is either because of my way of saying it like a pledge, or it is because of Ruby's way of listening to it like a witness. I can't decide.

Ruby, jewel in the mud, doesn't smoke, or do drugs. Ruby cries for trees. Many are passionate, but Ruby splits the very kernel of passion and pours its visionary juices in your eyes, see it feelingly. Ruby, the Aung San Suu Kyi of the protest movement, sears the hearts of bailiffs and sentences politicians to silence. Mr David Dwindle, MP, (Merchant Politician) local paymaster and national betrayer of the libdem environment hopes, can answer anyone except Ruby. Many come to fight their causes and go, many come and stay for good; Lisa-the-Lift and Rachel, Root and Pete and Jimmy-the-record, many are wondrous to me, but there is no one like Ruby. No one. She is the dream of my dogdays.

*

My beautiful Union Jack goes singingly at the top of my beautiful treehouse, natural architecture, more bowerbird than bauhaus. I saw the wood to fit snug around each branch, and set the platform floor with a bubble. There's a window and a little curtain made of writs. I carpet the walls and take three days chivvying the trap door to sit tight to its cradle. The comfy log holds by the burner, the smoke-burning stove, Root's invention. Root has to concretise and vaporise his ideas by turns. He makes the stove out of two Kwiksave family-size bean cans and the use of his incompleted PhD and spends most afternoons eddying around the canal in a home-made coracle, trying not to be seen by police, for he has been charged with the crime of sitting on a log humming Native American heart songs, and has been bailed off the route.

Root has a mind to put you on pause. It usually starts "have you ever wondered," and ends with stochastic and Newton-defying inventions. They say if you're down a deep well, looking up during daylight, the sky will be dark and the stars visible. This inadvertent starriness is what it must be like to be inside his mind, looking out. He doesn't see what we see; he sees both more and less, more stars, less daylight. The first time he tries to light his smoke-burning stove, he proves this in the negative. The twigs don't catch light but he sets fire to his dreads by mistake. Most people wouldn't.

More autumn. The treescape has a graphite beauty. This year could be the last year when it will have seasons at all, for a bypass knows no weather, it is always service-station no-time on a bypass.

*

The Monotonous Lark is the most boring bird in the whole wide world, and it is reincarnated in the person of Steven-the-

Grievance who has now taken up residence in my treehouse. I consider relocating. To Wimbly. There is no one there, at least to my knowledge, who lingers with such intent to commit an act of boredom upon my innocent person. Steven-the-Grievance is whining like an E flat in a G major chord because Reclaim the Streets has banned him from their meetings and Friends of the Earth central office won't make him director and Channel Four doesn't reply to his documentary proposal, "One Man's Sole Struggle Against the Newbury Bypass, and Against the Fascists Even Within The Protest Movement."

He wants me to join his society, called "Cry Oppression Against the Fascists Within The Movement." He founded it and it has one other member, an honorary member, Jason Johns, who mixed scamphood with shamanism to overthrow car culture, then got tired of painting his arse blue and living up a tree, and became the shadow Drugs minister for the Green Party. Stephen-the-Grievance one day hears Mr Jason Johns saying very nicely that he has never heard of this society. Steven-the-Grievance calls a retaliatory unscheduled meeting to summarily ban Mr Jason Johns from ever coming to meetings. He wants to hold this meeting in my treehouse.

"On principle," I say politely, "fuck off."

I am a spy for Jason's faction, he says.

"He has no sodding faction. Grow up. We're all on the same sodding side."

I am now the oppressor. I am a fascist. He blasts around for two hours, his face bright red, his T shirt maroon, whizzing around like a loganberry with a stick of dynamite shoved up its bum.

"Get out of my ear, I want to listen to my tree," I say. It is hopeless. He tells Ruby I'm a fascist.

"Oh grow up," says Ruby. "We're all on the same sodding side." Ruby is a fascist.

We ponder together. Ruby-the-delightful, ecology graduate and natural psychologist, borrows a typewriter and writes to Steven: thus. "The Independent, in receipt of your leaked proposal to Channel Four, wishes you to write a piece, 670,000 words, (exactly counted), on your opinions on local politics, drawing specifically on your personal experience and your detailed inner knowledge of Reclaim The Streets, Friends Of The Earth, Greenpeace, EarthFirst and COATFWTM. Please come to our offices in London and discuss this with L.O. Fairlop, (A.N.A.G.)"

Steven is dumb enough. I've met brighter dung-beetles.

Every time, these days, that I think of Ruby, I start myself panting, Dill the dog-like. But Ruby says she is wedded to the protest and insists nothing may come between them. I fervently agree and am therefore more than mildly - absolutely totally - gutted when Ralph lures her into his bender and they have a hand-fasting in Reddings Copse.

"Ralph," (this is me, rehearsing my hurt pride on my own,) "was just a premature ejaculation waiting to happen." I am obviously not above accidental oxymoron, so I omit to say this to Ruby. Anyway Ralph, King Da Rizla, rap artist, respect to the roots, is black rasta and I can't compete. Plus, he's older than me. Me, though, I grow old. Old in pity. I have matured in mercy, for this reason; I have learned to love what is fragile. In Wimbly I knew I hated the bullying coercion of consumer culture, its violence against nature, but there I only had an instinct to misbehave, an inarticulate unwillingness to co-operate, shoving my armchair in the street. Here, though, I identify with the victim, with nature, and feel within me the cruelty of the concrete master-race. I have taken a role in the tragic play, with maybe four hundred protester-protagonists, and maybe four hundred antagonists; security guards, bailiffs and police. This passion play has become more important than myself. And even more important than Ruby.

*

One morning in winter. I think it's November. This morning starts like any other. A few cars have arrived on site, donated, bust, for the protest, and are buried nose down in a circle; "Carhenge." They are being spraypainted on the side: Rust In Peace.

The woods are full of no noise except the mystifying devil-bird of music. Euan and Angus, tree musicians, use stethoscopes to play back the jazz-haunted riff of a tree in the wind. A tabor, pipes and fiddles play amongst the trees.

No one has left the fire for three days except to sign. There is a postbox for the giros, called "Number 2 the beeches." It's actually a wych elm, though I don't like to say. "Nice ash," says a visiting bog asphodel specialist, pointedly. That's the trouble with specialists. He knows the social history of the bog asphodel (only in Lancashire, only in the 19th century) but stumped if you ask him the difference between a banana and a slug pellet.

"Them on the brew get te giros all the same, but. Postman Pat disne ken either," says Rab the Weedjie poet down off of the M77 where he's wanted for reciting his poetry, which he's banned from doing under bail conditions.

A morning that starts like any other is exactly the morning you should know by now not to trust. Here he is, watch now the morning dressed in cheesy glasses and nasty mac, the morning you don't leave in charge of your kids. Such an morning. Freezing. We're all sitting round the fire waiting for the giro post. Jimmy-the-record ("I've got five different names and a criminal record in each") wants to tell anyone his story of the M11 campaign, and it's going to be hard listening to the brick by brick barricades, the railway sleeper and portcullis defences, the magically collapsible staircase, the oil drums full of water with which to flood out the bailiffs, and then at the top of the house, the gibbet where he was to hang himself, without wishing that this was the first time you'd heard it rather than the thirty first. Anyway, he was away doing his laundry at his mum's when the bailiffs came calling. The regret of it unhinged him a little, and he's been shy of the laundry basket since.

"That fire disne look the reet colour to me," says Rab. "It's no got enough pupple in it."

"Sorted," goes Stub, not the soul of sense, and tips an industrial tin of coffeemate into it. The flame, well-purple now, melts the tarp and when it solidifies it hangs like a sickly futurist legume and there's a serious hole. A morning like any other; well-brillig, but the slithy giros don't come. Instead, stiff letters come, identifying us as full-time protesters, not job seekers. The word "ineligibility" is used a lot. Ineligibility is a loathsome word, a coagulating word, barrier jelly, the contraception of our class system and of our nation state. Black or Tawny asylum seekers are ineligible. The Poor are ineligible. Travellers. Ineligible. Thorns in the flab of the Wimbly classes, who use the word as ineluctably as spermicide, inevitably you are ineligible, pass the nonoxynol 9 to rubber stamp our letterheads.

It's the first thing to unite everyone at the camp since Steven-the-Grievance left, and there was a vacuum of a shared loathing lost. A trade union emotion up-percolates around the fire. Four people leave immediately to pretend to look for work. They are the lucky ones, as it turns out.

Root, two fields away, is blowing his conch to the 11 o'clock dawn, blowing it to warm himself up. We think. In the end, he has to come running, mouth fuzzy like an emperor moth from blowing his conch too long. He was blowing it for real.

"There's six vans of security guards on their way. Fucking hopeless to warn you, it'd be faster to get the guys from the Rainbow Centre down."

"Come come," says Jimmy-the-record, "they've been waiting for a lift down here since 1962". He can't help it, he's a member of the exaggerati.

Ruby doesn't find Jimmy funny. She offers clingy cloying sympathy for those nicey nicey Wainbow Worriers. I think I've gone off her, since she bagged off with Ralph. I laugh loudly with Jimmy, just to check. She gives me a cold look, which amuses me more. I have. Oh, how the charismatic become routinised.

I wipe the smile off the face, mighty fast, for these guys are on business. There are a few security guards, but mostly it's bailiffs. They're here on a pre-emptive strike, to get us out before more of us arrive, making their job harder later.

The bailiffs set fire to the kitchen bender. They tip out all the food, and there's leeks and bananas in the canal for weeks afterwards. They get out knives and shred the tarps, they slash our climbing ropes and climbing harnesses. They grab Tash by the hair and pull her out of her bender where she is kipping. One of them gets his hand up her skirt and another rips off her shirt and squeezes her breasts and says "You not enjoying it? You a lessie?" She doesn't stop crying for three days and I can't get a hard-on for weeks in shame of my sex.

It's completely illegal. Who cares? It's viciously violent. Who sees?

We call the police, 999, from the mobile phone at 11.16. They do not arrive.

The bailiffs go for Pete when he's forty feet up in the air on a walkway, cutting the rope he's standing on. He's not roped to anything. He has to jump for a tree. He misses. He falls. He's hospitalised with back injuries.

Four of them together go for Jimmy-the-record until he vomits blood.

One of the bailiffs squeezes Rachel's hand onto his knife blade, cuts her hand to the bone, her scream slashes the very air to ribbons and he is smiling and squeezing it harder. And have I known cruelty before? Rachel's scream cuts so deep into the flesh of my mind, quick to the bone, so sensitises me never to forget, that any lesser pain heard since howls down that same wound. Never forget.

"Warn your friends," they say, "We'll be back."

Who needs vigilantes?

We phone the police again. They say they are on their way. We phone the press. No-one cares. We call the Guardian's Wit on Wednesday. He's not at his desk. He's recovering after three days last week working undercover as a Reliance Security guard, doing a front page exposé on Keith, their operations manager, for encouraging the guards to beat up protesters. ("Use kidney punches," says Keith. "They leave no bruises. Just don't get caught.")

Ruby calls me to the edge of the line of guards. Sliding behind a line of guards, thin as the evil which is thin as his lips; Keith himself. After the violence, it is very quiet around Keith. Me and Ruby and Keith and one camcordista, steady hands and level eyes, relentlessly filming him, filming his masonic ring, filming his masonic expression.

"You have been given a pay rise and promotion since last week," says Ruby. "How is that right?" No answer. "Why do you want us to get hurt?" she says. "Why?" Keith is evaporating.

"Stop," says the calm camcordista, soft. "You're on film. It's better to answer."

"We don't need to use violence," Keith says. (Mock-gentle voice, Caligula-pale eyes, cruelty come quiet-like.) "We can leave you and come spring, the rain will just gently wash you off the leaves into our arms. We'll take care of you. Good care."

This is it, the verbal equivalent of the kidney punch, the language which leaves no bruises. The courtesy of the language, and the cruelty of the eyes. This relation of courtesy and cruelty is the marriage of sadism. Even Ruby doesn't know how to reply to it.

They are all gone at 12.57. The police arrive, punctual, at full saunter speed at 13.15. (It has taken one hour and fifty nine minutes. When we need three ambulances, for Pete, for Jimmy and for Rachel, they can get here in 7, 13, and 11 minutes respectively.)

The police line runs thus: it's nothing to do with us, but you can bring a private case against the bailiffs if you wish. If you think you can afford it. Then one of them, a wringy little person, a milk and two veg sort of man, makes a statement about police impartiality, tough on crime, tough on criminals, objective, strong, firm policing. Jimmy-the-record laughs sarcastically. He is arrested and given bail conditions which forbid him being anywhere on the bypass route.

The nights are full of threat now and the days are knife wary. Genuine vigilantes come, shooting at us with shotguns, threatening us on the CB, "They should be burned down in thar trees." "Nah, thar too green ta barn." Chainsaws start whining on parts of the route, snagging my nerves. The weather comes grim winter at us. "It's miserable out there," says a voice from the communal bender. "Well let's go and cheer it up." (It's the only halfway funny thing that happens in the whole of December.) I spend a day cloud-counting, hoping to amuse the anorak in me, but it leaves me feeling vasty as if I'd swallowed too much air.

I am low now, at the low of the fallen year. All I know of the outside world is the pubs which ban us, and shops which won't serve us. A legal system both bent from outside and bending from within, to criminalise us. The police who will not protect us from assault. MI5 and Brays Private Detectives who constantly spy on us. We read portraits of ourselves in the pages of the Daily Express. We are drugged to the eyeballs and wallowing in our own excrement. Our vehicles should be destroyed, and we should be sprayed with a dye, disqualifying us from welfare for a year. That should teach us some respect. This last in the italics of a hysterical grin. It is signed by one Mr McWhinney. Mr McWhinney has quite grown up.

If people support us, they're very, very quiet out there. I'm doing this for everyone, and everyone doesn't give a shit. My voice falls dead on the felt walls of a sound-proofed room, and one way quiet is a horrible thing. It makes me think too much without the ventilation of an audience. Truth and lies. Me, Ruby, Root and four hundred pesky galileos saying the world can't revolve around the car. Truth and lies. A road is beautiful progress, a car is a beautiful companion. Lies are expensive to produce. Truth comes free. Car adverts and cars are the expensive lie. Traffic fumes and asthma come free. Something for nothing. Hurry, hurry, hurry for your free cancers, your free pollution, your free car crashes. On all pavements near you today.

When I think of the road, I think of more and more monoculture of more and more suburbia. What I do, I'm doing in defiance of the Louis Queasy Chintzy, the sickly stale air of suburban car culture. I want the fresh air of nature, the lifefull wind of the French revolution. Here I am, storming the Bastille, to release the *publique générale* from the jail of ever more roads, ever more traffic, and what do I find but that the *publique générale* is just seven thick old men, blind as bog rolls, who don't want to leave their prison.

*

Mum and Dad come to see me near Christmas, and they bring me a state of the sleep sleeping bag, a radio with about a thousand batteries, the Sunday Telegraph, sixteen tins of tuna and a thermal vest. It takes me twenty minutes to persuade them to come up to my treehouse, where they seem more impressed by my domestics than my politics, particularly Root's burner.

"It's awfully clever," says Mum, "and you wouldn't get away with it in Wimbly."

Dad spends an hour in private audience with the stove and I wish Root himself would show up. Or Shortstuff, or Lisa-the-Lift, or Rachel or Ruby or anyone except Stub. Up my rope comes Stub, stoned, smirky, bad breath and a biro sign on his teeshirt saying "You can't tell me anything about a security guard that's too stupid to be true." It took him the whole of last week to write.

"Those security guards - " Mum is drawing in a breath which she is going to spend on saying "It's a job and someone's got to -" when Stub says "Ja get me teeshirt? You carn tell me -" but forgets the end of it and asks Mum to read it off his back for him. She doesn't, and Stub starts reading the Telegraph upside down.

Dad concentrates other people's minds wonderfully. "And you," he says, with all due mockery, "are presumably not the brightest of bulbs in the chandelier of life?" Since Dad thinks he'll have to take out a second mortgage if he spends more than twenty words a day, he chooses them with great care. Stub takes less notice of Dad than Dad is used to; his eyes are now shut, he is using a climbing harness as a pillow, and is trying to suck Mum's toe.

"Are You On Drugs?" says Mum.

It's sweet, oh the little lamb, all things bright and beautiful, how long have I been older than my mother? Stub goes into hysterics and Mum goes crimson. Dad goes pearshaped and Stub leaves. It's the first sensible thing he's done since he put out a fire in a bender by pissing on it. Still he started the fire in the first place.

"We had tea with Mr McWhinney," says Mum, into the ineluctable family chasm. "He's running for parliament. And he hasn't forgotten the hogweed. I stuck up for you, Roddy, I said hogweed's not so bad, and well by Jove have you seen comfrey?"

Bless her, she'd never make an activist.

Dad hears what I didn't say. He's uncannily canny like that.

"You call yourself an activist, then?"

I pretend that my eyes are glazing over, *non comprendo*, sir. Does he mean "so you fink you're so smart" or does he mean, "so you're actually doing something useful"? Does he approve or disapprove? I take the risk.

"Look, Dad," I say, "when I came here, I wanted my freedom - a bit of space. Now, though, it's got so much bigger than me. It's like the whole idea of freedom, every kind of freedom, is under threat, doesn't matter if it's nature being ripped up so there's no free countryside to walk in, or the CJA or whatever, and Twyford Down was -"

"Ah," goes Dad, "it was a stitch up. The E.U. dropped its action against the British Government. Twyford Down was a deal for Maastricht and we live in an effing police state but you've still got to get an effing job, end of the day, I'm not running an effing hotel whenever you feel like coming back."

"Darling," says Mum in reproach at him saying "effing" in front of me, but me, I'm absolutely gobsmacked, totalled, and I have a massive desire to hug him, which of course would be such a shock to us both that he'd have a coronary toot sweet.

"Eh, well, 'nuff said," goes Dad, getting up to go. And, no, it isn't anything like 'nuff, but sometimes you've got to be satisfied.

They are leaving. Dad is half-way down the rope, out of ears. Mum hangs back a second. "By the way, dear, I do think you're right about the road and so does your father, but for pity's sake don't let him know I said that. I think he's almost proud of you, though it's always hard to tell."

I sob. I wait till she's gone, as you do, then I sob like a child.

*

January. I wake most mornings with a terrible attack of morning thickness, but I channel this energy, it fuels my eviction-preparations. I wrap the tree in barbed wire, spike it with staples to blunt chainsaws and build a second walkway. I think about taking a mattock to my treeroots, to hack some of the roots in two so if the tree is felled, it will fall unpredictably. If it isn't felled, it will recover. I get no further than thinking about it. Shortstuff and I make a net, a web of ropes and steel cables, stretched hanging between six trees, so one person can protect all of them by lying in this internet.

Shortstuff - so named, of course, for his being six foot seven, and girthed wide as Serbian expansionism - gives everyone tubs of lard for the eviction; "You lard your wrists and they can't catch hold of you," he goes.

I prepare a larder - an eviction stash - in the corner of my treehouse. (My deceased grandmothers both take a peep through the chromosomal net curtains; he gets it from me, says one. "I very much doubt it. Thinking ahead and a sensible diet? Granary loaves and pine nuts? He gets it from me.")

I feel ready, on yer toes ready, and I am tender to the motto Be Prepared, because, prepared, your future is like a sculpture, clay of tomorrow, moist in your palm. Live like this, damp side out to the world. It's all I'd tell my kids; live generously and keep the clay wet.

*

February, still wet and freezing. My sexual weather is about a hundred per cent humidity. Wring it out like a flannel, morning and night, and it's wet again instantly.

I still need to sort the lock-on points in my tree. I request the advice of Lock-on Lindy. Lock-on Lindy despises me, I feel, for she is a fundamentalist, a born-again protester. She has submerged her feelings, diluted them in the communal pond.

But there is something about her I can't work out. She wears the dreads and the beads, the climbing harness and the one tatty glove, (colourless, fingerless, made from the runt wool of a particularly pitiful sheep), but none of this is enough to mask the IKEA in her, bossy black-china voice, self-assembly wooden specs, eyebrows in a straight line like a checkout queue, square hands like plastic shopping baskets.

Lock-on Lindy is the duty officer of D locks, and what she doesn't know about delay isn't worth knowing. She performs time and immobility studies, our time, versus their immobility. Putting into the calculations the cost of locks, plus the cost of arrest (the pricey bit in our equations) and balance these against the delay and consequent cost to the other side.

I watch her once, asked to do an on-site cost-benefit analysis, mid-eviction. You think she hasn't heard. She stays motionless. Her mind moves like a lizard over these rocky places. You might see dry figures and sandy numbers. To a lizard, it's teeming with life. She goes the zig zag from one invisible juicy zero to another succulent digit. Twenty eight seconds later, comes the print-out. With one casualty, plus us on lunchtime news, means donations up by £550. Expenditure three D-locks, (£100) and £25 on concrete lock-ons, and three arrests. Three hours to release us costs £4,999.87. This represents wise use of resources.

Lock-on Lindy visits my tree. "One hook embedded in a concrete sleeve around the branch and a D-lock round your neck. £40 to us and £750 to them and say sorry to your tree," she snaps.

"Is the patronism extra?"

"I'm a consultant."

Yorkshire Water is run by people like you, I tell her. She gulps, mullet-like. She has got feelings, and I am ashamed. I offer her thirty eight packets of yoghurt-coated raisins and some soya dessert, (apple flavoured.) (Why is every road protest swimming in soya dessert, (apple flavoured)? I have never so much as smelt it before. This is a deeper mystery than numerology to me.)

I overhear her talking to Ruby later, their voices clear as hock across twenty feet of cold night.

"He's only here because he fancies you."

"He doesn't even like me. Not anymore, anyway," Ruby lies.

"He does. Anyone can see." Bitter. "He isn't committed to the protest, he's just here for you." There is a pause. Two trees apart, me and Rube hit the same thought at the same moment.

"You're pretty into him yourself."

"I'm not." (Lock-on Lindy lies.) "OK, I am a bit." (Lowers voice.) "I understand him. I'm from Wimbly myself."

Vinyl, draylon, formica, plastic catalogues and mug trees, Brent Cross Shopping City.

"Ooh, how lovely," (Ruby, here, ignorant as chewing gum.)

Where does this leave me? Ruby that I once adored, adores Ralph. Lock-on Lindy who likes me, makes my instincts curl with horror like plastic press-on wood-effect lino. I am stuck between a Wimblyite and a Donga. Caught between the plastic ornamental heron and the lyretailed nightjar. And I am more of a sparrow, me. A country sparrow.

"You do like him."

"No," lies Lindy, "I don't. He doesn't do anything communal, he doesn't have any idea of how to share, he eats alone, he stays up his tree. He doesn't even begin to get the point of a community."

"Give him time," says Ruby, candlevoiced, "he wants to convert."

Someone starts playing a mandolin and I hear no more. Conversion. The very word is my agony and my desolation. My soul is lonely and I long to belong, but, belonging, I leave my carping, pisstake, warped as I please, creased and complicated self neatly folded outside the church door and come in naked and nice as a bodyshop-coconut breeze. I was born liminal, wanting in, wanting out, cursed by my dilemmic desires.

There's nothing like hearing yourself discussed for making you question yourself. What am I here for, anyway? To save the planet or to get my rocks off? To live selfless and communal or to forge my identity in the smithy of a road protest? To be the conscience of a nation or just to get away from Wimbly for a while? All I'm sure of is that I have known, here, the sweetness of freedom as I never have before, Van Gogh freedom, gold flowers exploding through the paint into suns of freedom.

I comfort myself with DIY civil engineering. I never would have thought it had the pulling power, but there is nothing in this world so wonderful as a piece of civil engineering. It is the essence of both the Renaissance and the Resistance, it is both science and art, the work of the amateur and professional, both cavalier and exactly planned, both logorithmic and utopian. Everything which is good seems so fragile, and everything which is bad so powerful, until you apply some uncivil engineering to the affair.   .

The camp next to this one has an underground system of catacombs and tunnels, but here it is too boggy. Instead we have a vision of a dam of dams. It takes two days to dam up a nearby stream just below the camp and flood the area to slow down the cherrypickers' access - to stop them coming in to take us out. It is a lyrical dam and durable. An act of love, a political effect and a theatrical statement. We christen the camp Anarchipelago. It works a treat; everywhere gets waterlogged, Lord Quag gives a groggy salivary grin and admits he couldn't have done better himself, and two police officers on the spy for pixie work are personally amused and professionally pissed off.

Rumour now comes visiting, insistent, dogged as a poll tax collector, whispering one word: Eviction.

Eviction in the mass enrolment of criminals and journalists into the ranks of security guards. Eviction in the way the police and bailiffs start to look more and more like cars; their riot shields like windowscreens, their helmets and visors like sun roofs. The police often have their number plates on their shoulders, though when things get rough, they do seem to cover them up.

Eviction is written in the frost. Eviction hangs in the frozen mists on the canal, eviction in the posture of the wickermen, eviction in the cracked wheat frozen onto the wholemeal pasta, eviction on the CB and the mobile phone, eviction in the frequency of press visits, and of police scouts and of security guard recruitment, in the failure of one after another of our legal challenges.

Eviction in me too, where it calls itself resolve. Eviction in Shortstuff where it calls itself strength, eviction in Martin and Moira where it calls itself something old fashioned like honour and valour and courage.

Eviction is in the air like a coming season, and eviction actually replaces spring. Here there is no spring in the air, no upthrust in no leaves, no goforthness in no sapling, no vigour in no sun, no green in no chlorophyll, no burgeoning chissick in no baby bird. It is the coldest winter, temperatures are down to minus 14, and it stays below freezing until May. Here for us, there is no spring, and it is a killing thing to the beg of the spirit.

Eviction notices come through for our camp. The wires are humming with rumour; eviction now, tomorrow, yesterday. Someone sends out the aruga, an alarm call to all tree-respecters. One morning, so cold my lips have frozen onto my sleeping bag zip, and the snow is settling - in the fire - one morning comes not eviction, but Haggle.

She arrives the day the first security guard cordon surrounds the camp. I do not see her, as I have locked-on to my sleeping bag, but Haggle FM broadcasts to the guards - "COME AND GET US IF YER FINK YER TALL ENERF."

At about four, in the dusk, I catch a glimpse of her. Orange face, green glasses, green and orange dreads, orange teeshirt and green shorts - in the coldest January since 1946. Haggle, fat as righteous indignation, loud as belated justice and compelling as a trumpet solo. She is nature to the grub, no tea cosies, no Tiscoes on her, she is nettles, tidal waves, Pinatubo. She is as monstrous and resplendent in appetite as Giant Hogweed. This is it. Ecce Hogweed. She is Giant Hogweed made flesh and living in the tree next door to me.

She is Hildegaard of Bingen and Boadicea, she is Edith Sitwell and Grendel's mother. She is both Pankhursts and Yeats' crazy salad, she is feminism from 1968 to 1979, (including Australian but excluding French,) and the entire movement for electoral reform. She is an prodigious woman and the one who will make off with my manhood. This is Woman and what am I? Terrified.

Haggle puts up an impromptu broadcasting tower in the tree, and we share a rope walkway between the two trees. Jed, till now the eloquence of the camp, with the bored authority of a teacher to assembled class of lazy security guards, "you're overexposed to violence and underexposed to thought," "ten years' graduate unemployment and what do you get? Road protests," Jed, whose voice comes back off half of Berkshire, Jed is but a whisper beside Haggle on her tower. Haggle, Gob made manifest on this earth, Mouf FM, getting a thunderous echo off the very vault of heaven. "YER OBSOLETEYER. YER A CHILD OV MUVVER NATECHER - SURPRISED SHE DUZAN HATECHER."

I cannot pluck up the courage to speak to her. I've waited all my life to meet this woman, I can wait, I tell myself, and postpone my pleasure, save my chips till I've ate my scrambled egg. It is a lie. Truth, like male virginity, is revealed in the knees. Mine are shaking like sea squirts.

*

!@&*$ Every morning. Every fucking morning. CB's at dawn, shooting up their panic down the veins. Every day, the dodgems, they leave, we leave. The security guard coaches leave Chieveley service station, we follow in cars. Bailiffs and police leave at four or five. Cracking the can of dawn open before they're out of the offie of night. I go routescouting, following them, radioing back from the car to the Third Battle office, saying where they are, giving the O.S. grid reference number. My last message goes something like this: "They're turning left now, could be Go-Tan today, they're reversing, looking for something, someone, don't know. Oops. Think it's me. Over."

They ask my name.

"We've got a lot of footage of you at various camps. The address 33 Acacia Avenue mean anything?" (Fuck.) "Acacia Avenue, Wimbly?"

"Yes, occifer." Fast apology. "I'm dyslexic."

"And cheeky." He is breathing very fast for a policeman.

"Yes. And cheeky with it."

"We're pretty tired of you lot following us around."

"Yes. I'm tirribly sirry." (Best Wimbly.)

"We've got an eye on you."

They get me to empty my pockets and they find nothing. They take down details of the car and check its tax and insurance. It's quite creamy with legality.

"You're unner arrest."

For fucking what? "For what?"

"For wasting police time." Comes the wit.

"We are arresting you on suspicion of intent to obstruct police and bailiffs in the lawful carrying out of their duties."

I like the police. I am snug in the car between two officers in uniform. I wonder if I'm gay. I think of Haggle. No, I just like the police.

"I've never been in trouble before," I say, conversationally, "I like the police." I wait for one of them to say "Got a right one 'ere, Serge," like on The Bill, but they don't. One of them just says "shut the fuck up." That's the trouble with the police -they don't watch The Bill. I do not always like the police.

I am taken to the station and charged and given the Newbury sausage.

The duty officer is a wee boiled sweet of a woman, her face half cheek half cherry. "It means that under your bail conditions, you're not allowed anywhere on the bypass site. Be on your way, and you'll not be back." Something incontrovertible going on here. I do not controvert. Uncharacteristically wise.

I speak to a lawyer on the phone. He's irate with it. "It's a question of attacking civil liberties they use bail conditions as a political tool it's quite outrageous I'm going to write to The Times about it I'm taking up this issue with my MP I will not let this drop I've been practising in law for twenty three years and I've never seen anything like this I will rise to the challenge I will pursue these cases to the very towering height of the European Courts of Human Rights I will rise - " the rest of his sentence is lost in the thunderous applause in his mind and I can hear it even over the phone, he rises from the bench in ermine and curls for my Lord Chief Justice for My Lady Mercy, applause roars, he, lion-like, roars himself hoarse to the pride of Lincolns Inn.

"Oh and another thing." (Duty Officer. Voice half cherry juice, half cyanide, I had not got her measure before.) "You'll have to sign at the police station every day."

I can cope.

"In Wimbly."

I can't cope.

I call my lawyer back but he is on leave of outrage. "He's too angry to speak. It's his righteous indignation, plays him up worse than his bad back," says the switchboard plugged to full chat. "You don't want to give indignation too much of a welcome, as Heraclitus says." She's wasted on a switchboard. Who isn't?

So. My choice. Wimbly or on the run. What would you? I'm on the run. If I'm seen on the route I can be arrested and immediately imprisoned. I have to scarf up and stay away from the police. I hate this.

Mum sees me on the news one day and the next time I phone her she says: "You look awfully sinister, dear, with a scarf over your face. I think it puts people off." I love her "people." Her "people" all live on Acacia Avenue, are very, very nice and have a son called Roddy, Roddy? RODDY. Innocent self-extrapolation is just a beautiful thing. I like my mum.

I daydream. I am in prison. Dad is there, gigantic-like, huge breath in, "HE'S OUR SON NAFF OFF" and he bellows a whole northwesterly force ten through these five words. The police flutter dying-like to the floor, like the losing blue rosettes in the wind of the coming general election. I like my dad.

*

The camp is being decorated, the trees dressed for eviction. There is a banner down the side of my tree: "We'll fight them in the beeches." Intentional. Ruby wakes me up horribly betimes one morning to help her unwrap a new banner over the walkway. "Why destroy beaty?" it says, unintentionally.

"They don't see this place as beautiful," she says, pointing to patrols of fluorescent guards doing clearance work nearby. "Look at them, in their ugly uniforms, their ugly jobs, their ugly machines. By being here, they have already made this place ugly so what does it matter to them if they destroy it? They have brought the ugliness with them."

This is quintessentially absolutely Rubyesque. My summer passion blushes me again.

Ruby is an English garden, Ruby is honey stone walls suckling lavender beds. Ruby is a barefoot lawn, roses rising in a chamomile dawn. Haggle, though, is ungardenable. Haggle is the fuck off I'm a wilderness, mandrake and monkey orchid, warty toad, razor strop fungus and the stinkhorn mushroom. Ruby is all Greensleeves and drink to me only with thine eyes. Haggle is the raw growl before poetry existed. I could not love one so much, if I didn't love the other equally.

*

Every morning. Every fucking morning. Someone's trying to chivvy the CB but it's being jammed by Newbury vigilantes, humming vitriol on the wires; truckies, local wideboys, and assorted hostages to hate. Some viggies shoot at Shortstuff as he hangs off a tripod for sixteen days and nights, some firebomb the protest camp at Rickety Bridge.

This morning is a morning for only getting occasional crackles. "The convoy is close to you and closer."

"Aruga" goes Stub, as he does every morning.

"ARUGAAAAAAA," goes Haggle, this morning, as she never has before.

There's a Donga on the drums, veteran of Twyford Down, wearing the war paint of Twyford chalk. Root is blowing his conch. Bagpipes knot the sinews in the very air.

"ARUGA GET FUCKING LOCKED ON." (Lock-on Lindy, fearing loss of investment.)

Jimmy-the-record goes for the underwater lock-on point, under ice, this morning. Robski and someone I don't know climb to the top of a tree with their mountain bikes and D-lock on.

A cordon of security guards surrounds the camp. Four people - old ladies, locals, - try to bust the cordon and are arrested. Nicely arrested and apologetically, because security guards and police hate roughing up old ladies. With fifty really lacy old ladies, you could hold up a road for months.

"COME AND GET ME IF YOU DARE". (Haggle FM)

And then comes my vision, my vision busting the security cordon of heaven itself. Haggle, green hair, green glasses, green body-paint, Haggle, standing on top of her treehouse shaking the branches in the fury of the primeval swamp, Haggle, stark fucking naked and covered in lard.

Have I never known admiration.

Have I never paid homage.

The clouds have halted, the gods are gawping and I have forgotten how to breath in.

Respect.

*

Someone's pulling at the rope up to my treehouse. It's Root. He comes up, closely followed by Ruby. I see Stub stumbling about by the communal bender and making a run for my rope. The idea of being stuck with Stub in a siege appals me. I try to yank up the rope but he gets to it first. It's close - he's being chased by a bailiff, and Stub's having trouble getting onto the rope. This is comeuppance for a git like Stub who never practised his prussick knots. Stub's up five foot on the rope now and swinging around like a pissed pendulum, his boots about the level of the bailiff's face. The bailiff backs off and my heart sinks.

I see Shortstuff. He is prowling outside the security cordon, crashing like a grizzly denied its tamarind. He climbs a tree outside the cordon, and no one takes any notice. Then he starts climbing from tree to tree, climbing higher, up forty foot now seventy, and across three trees which takes him well over the guards' line, now he's a hundred feet up and across eight trees, and he is underneath Haggle's treehouse. He has not seen Haggle, and she hasn't seen him.

The wild green volume-monger lets belt: "IT'S WEDNESDAY. THAT'S WODENSDAY. WE LIKE WODENSDAY."

Shortstuff looks up in sheer amazement. She must be some view from where he is, and Shortstuff loses his grip and falls, caught by good luck, in the internet. A cherrypicker (a crane) with two bailiffs is ready nearby.

Stub takes the piss bucket and tips it over them, before anyone can stop him. Stub is the brew crew minority of the movement, he is himself the yellow peril, the uric acid of the body politic. I sigh for all of us. This sigh is the first collective action of my entire life.

He starts making up to Ruby. "Course I could take on six. Give them a good kicking. They're fucking terrified of me. They don't mess with me. I'm Stub, me, and they know it."

Ruby, beautiful to me today, is watching out for Shortstuff while half-listening to Stub. Rivulets, streamlets in her voice, smooth grow the rushes oh, murmurs without paying any attention, playing beguileless begandhi to Stub's bumptious bejehoshaphat.

Then, horribly, Ruby screams.

"Are you hurt? What's wrong?" I shout in panic. "What's -"

"No. Not me. Shortstuff. Sorry - no - look - what - I can't - NO NO DON'T DON'T DON'T DO THAT-" She is ripping her fingers to blood on the bark, and from where I am, I can't see, so I struggle to climb three branches. Then I see, and it sickens.

The cherrypicker has reached Shortstuff in the internet. The bailiffs have riot shields. One bailiff turns his shield on end and, using the edge as a blade, strikes at Shortstuff on the head. His forehead streams with blood. He doesn't even lift his hands to defend his head. The bailiff continues, repeatedly. He is smiling the smile of cruelty. Shortstuff is also smiling, smiling the smile of saints in statues.

Down below, the gathering crowd has now seen. There is a scream from them all, but their scream floats lost and ineffective. What does the bailiff care about the crowd? Ruby is in tears. Shortstuff has moved into serenity. He keeps his little private

Valhalla, like a place of retreat, for moments such as this. He is now handcuffed to the cherrypicker and taken out. On the way down, the bailiffs, (both, this time,) lay into him, kicking him in the shins, and kidney punching him over and over. One hundred and fifty police officers on site and not one lifts a finger to prevent it.

I realise I am crying. I am crying because Shortstuff is hurt. I am also crying because I feel fragile and afraid and betrayed, for here, the police don't even pretend to be objective or honest, because my mother told me aged two I could trust them and my experience tells me aged two and twenty I can't. I feel childish and simple and naïve and I'm crying for the loss of my civic innocence.

Not much stirs below and there is relative calm. We are in the interval of this passion play of ours.

Shortstuff is given a chargesheet and is not allowed to see a doctor although he is peeing blood and his head is still streaming. The bailiffs are given a teabreak and a Mars Bar and a nice smile from the Central Office of Information Press Officer, Lisley. I tune to Radio Berkshire for the news. We figure for a minute in a vox pop. Who saw what happened to Shortstuff?

All the legal observers agreed, as did the Channel Four cameras, and BBC TV. The Independent saw, and The Wit on Wodensday. Even the Newbury news reporter. Did one hundred and fifty police officers on site see anything similar? Not one. The vox pop checks. Someone asks thirty police officers. None of them saw. Not one. Thirty more? Nope.

The bailiffs are behind schedule with everything. The Undersheriff of Berkshire has a meeting with the bailiffs, chief of police, and Lisley. The Undertaker is checking his watch against Lisley's clipboard. It makes me nervous. The importance of speed and schedule, to them, means the increased likelihood of our injury. Lisley is a fascination to me. She is watching Haggle and laughing at her, with the mean little mouth of self-elected superiority. How is it possible for anyone - let alone Lisley - to think they are superior to Haggle? Lisley; mouth like a stapler, eyes like paper clips, expression like the office stationery budget. More than jobsworth, she has been there at all state-endorsed acts of evil, the little biro of bureaucracy, ticking it off, satisfactorily completed, she was there, from the Crusaders' slash-and-burn path of rape and murder, to Mussolini's memo-writing, she was there in Tiananmen Square, she is everywhere in Burma today, ticketyboo for SLORC, she is the original, pat pending PR endorsement for state-hate from the beginnings of time to now.

Everything is getting its marching orders. Cameras start snapping around on all sides, press cameras, cameras for the Highways Agency, Reliance Security cameras, police cameras and one blazoning MI5 purely by virtue of its being the only unmarked camera. (MI5, of course, in the too-short peace interlude in Ireland, is doing its target practice on road protesters.) It is MI5 that gets the best shot of Stub - him with his fingers down his throat trying to vomit his last five cans of Tennents over a bailiff.

The drums drum on. Bagpipes do their Bruegel bit undeterred. The cherrypicker is up and running, closing in. There are only two trees left now, mine and Haggle's, and one rope walkway, the one that runs between us, a hundred and fifty feet in the air. The chainsaw geezer is cutting away the branches of my tree. Ruby is pleading with him. "Give her one," is his only response. Root is leaning on a branch, writing. They saw off the branch he is leaning on. Ruby and I both lurch towards him.

"Don't worry, I was roped on," he says in a scrap of a voice and, sure enough, a little twilly rope, granny-knotted onto a twig, sticks up from the back of his trews. But his lips are pale. It has unstrung both their nerves so when the bailiffs arrive, they don't even try to get out onto the walkways. They are taken down together in a cherrypicker. Stub is taken out next. Halfway down he succeeds in vomiting. On his own sock.

I am standing on the top of my treehouse, hoping desperately that I'm not going to need a crap. I hear a swollen-neck cry from the crowd below, and I can't work out what it's for. Then, suddenly, my whole tree shakes in a death rattle. I know what the crowd is on about; they are cutting this tree down, with me still in it. They can't be. I look at my watch. Half past four. They've got thirty minutes to get these last two trees, because if they work after five they have to start paying overtime. Cutting it down is quicker than sending up a cherrypicker to get me out. They can't be doing this. They can.

I don't think I have the spring in my hind legs to get from the treehouse roof to the walkway, but I do. My body is streaming sweat and my hands are slipping off the ropes. I look down the trunk of my tree; there it is, threequarters cut through and swayful as a voter. I'm fucked. When my tree goes, it will pull down this walkway I'm stood on. I can't move. There is terror all around me, and it has turned the very air to monosodium glutamate. I cannot push through it. I jerk myself four steps towards Haggle's tree. I'm near but not near enough. My tree is going - I jerk four more - the crowd is roaring me to move faster, and I can't do anything but jerk - I jolt along four more steps - my tree is going over - I am going to fall.

Caught. How Haggle catches me is the world's latest miracle; one arm through my armpits and she throws a sling round my waist to strap me like a baby chimp to the side of its mother tree. The walkway twirls away like bunting in the breeze.

Then. My tree, falling, (twist of fate? it read my mind), doesn't fall straight and crashes, unpredictably, right across the cherrypicker.

Haggle, fistfuls of branches, howls below, "NATECHER HATES YER. YOU MESS AROUND WITH TREES AND THEY'LL MESS AROUND WITH YOU. YOUR MACHINE'S BEEN FUCKED BY A TREE IN ANCESTORLAND."

Everything stops. All on hold. Very quiet downstairs. I smell terrible. It's fear-sweat, unlike any other kind. Bittersick smell. "Hang on in there, you little darling," says Haggle. I want my mum but Haggle will do just fine. My near-death has shocked the crowd. Sensible crowd is silenced by fear. The cherrypicker's death has silenced the bailiffs. The Undertaker eats his sandwiches in silence. Then I feel the bubbly pressure of an old habit; the result of terror turned silly. It's the only sound for miles. In all this silence, all eyes on me, dignity and I part company for good, me immobile, glued to the side of the tree and giggling like a shrimp.

It's too late in the day for the Undertaker to get another cherrypicker down to the site, so he can't evict Haggle and me. He is in spiteful mood, you can see it in his chin and elbows. He hurls away his sarnie, and holds council. A decision is taken.

He sends up two climbers to our tree. One has a chainsaw strapped to his back.

"Afternoon," they say to me, just below the treehouse on their way up. Haggle climbs back to the very top branches.

The climbers throw out Haggle's water container, all her food saved as eviction stash, her bedding and her ropes to descend. I hear them laugh over something. They wave her clothes like a trophy to the hostile and jeering crowd, and throw the clothes to the ground. Then the climbers break down the walls of her treehouse but not the platform which is too secure, and anyway it's five minutes to five. As they go down the tree, they cut, meticulously, each branch flush to the trunk.

"That's you sorted," says one of the professional climbers. Well, the lingo. Looking at him, he could be one of us. Twenties, climbing harness, hair in dreads. Betraying the dread philosophy, there's a price on each dreadlock.

Betraying the philosophy of the climbing community, too, Judas is a name he is now familiar with. He bought a car with his massive earnings, but the day he drove it out the garage, he drove it into a tree. Natural justice is best meted out by nature.

He is right. It is us well-sorted. No food, water, bedding or means of descent. For Haggle, no clothes. This is a fucker of a night. The damp in the air even now predicts it'll be another minus ten night tonight and all the surrounding trees have been cut down so the winds cut mean like wet whips.

The fluorescent army of security guards leaves. The police leave, and the bailiffs and climbers. The Undertaker of Berkshire leaves. The crowd doesn't leave for ages. The cherrypicker has to be towed away, as my tree has damaged the controls.

After an hour, there are a lot of people still stood around the tree, there's a lot of not-knowing-what's-to-be-done to be done. Loudhailer Jerry offers to get John-the-Bowman out of the Clocktower, the only pub which serves protesters. John-the-Bowman has a great skill. He ties rope to string and string to arrow and shoots this arrow over a branch so someone can climb up and start building a treehouse or a walkway. But tonight, here, he shakes his head. It's too high for him and we're too exposed to be sure of his aim. Self-skewered protesters would be something of an own goal. Everyone leaves.

I untie the sling slowly and crawl cautious up to the platform. Dusky. Silent up here. Haggle, slowly, comes down. Even Giant

Hogweed can feel pain, pain of exposure, of cold and of cruelty. Her exuberance is crushed and I hate to see it. Her face is small and nearly snivelly. I try desperately not to look at her naked body, turning away when she gets closer. This is the moment, after all, which I have panted for, me and she alone in a tree. I think of all the ringing things I would have said to her yesterday. Now I just mumble, "D'you want a go on my duffel coat?"

She tries to say thanks, but her voice doesn't come.

"V'you lost your voice?" I go. She goes: "Mmm."

I can't think of anything to say. At all.

She's wearing my coat now and my socks but she's still shivering so I give her my hat. And my boots and my scarf. I look at her. Her green paint has come off her face and she's gone a lilac white. I give her my jumper, and let her smoke my last. She's lost and young and scared and cold. I hate it, I hate to see it. It's like seeing your parents cry when you're a kid. I'm choked, tell the truth.

"Gi's a hug," she goes, "I feel like shit."

Holding her, I feel a fierce tenderness. It's the savage desire to protect something that I feel for nature. I hold her all night. We don't even kiss.

We chill out a bit. We chill out a lot. I think Haggle cried in the night, because in the morning there was ice on her cheeks.

*

And here we are, in the political nick, the salon de refusés. Haggle has pneumonia in the medical wing at Holloway. Ruby is next to her, her interviews to the press are lark-ascending appeals to the world. In Bullingdon prison, I've been done for aggravated trespass and Shortstuff is on a food and water strike. Root is humming American heart songs three cells away from me. His conch has been confiscated lest the walls of HMP Jericho fall when he blows it. Stub is the only one let off. (He's just an ordinary hooligan, says the magistrate, and he doesn't belong in prison.)

Who else isn't here? The vigilantes who shot at us, although the police know who they are. The Newbury two who firebombed Loudhailer Jerry's bus with petrol bombs. And they are free, for although they were brought to court, and although they admitted doing it, they were released. Congratulated and released. The bailiffs who assaulted us are free. Promoted and free. The politicians who broke their own environmental protection laws are free as London pigeons, free to peck up sick and shit on the homeless. And those who have clear-felled the country, the thee you vowed to, and ah but they go free as the tumbleweedseed to blow.

And me, my freedom hurts me again. Here, the square room and leccy, the air-conditioned McAir, McAches my head to crashing. My headache is churning concrete, there's boiling tarmac under my eyelids, so I can barely see. Some marauding haulage contractor is mocking my pain and a Costains work team is laying a road base over my temples. There are JCB's in my throat and a kanga drill judders through my arms. I used to have moorlands inside me, now I have concrete within. It's the worst they have done, they have robbed me of my inner freedom, my free landscape. And of my free future, for even when we are released, we will never be free, as MI5 and private detectives keep files on us all, to punish us freely and forever with nameless fears.

All you can lose your freedom for, since the Criminal Justice Act. For humming. For being under suspicion of intent to hum. For sitting in trees. For walking too slowly. For saying "fuck" in the presence of a fucking police officer. For objecting when the government itself acts illegally. For having a party for more than twenty people. For reciting poetry. For drumming. For being a Traveller. For sleeping outdoors.

All I wanted was my freedom. Freedom to breath my own sky-air, freedom for nature to *naturans* freely in, freedom for movement to walk freely in, freedom for the sycamorewood, the ashwood and the oakwood to grow free in, freedom not to have all of England under concrete, Wimblified, freedom to sleep in the woods on softly softly beechnuts.

All I wanted was to be free as cuckoo-spit and conker-shine, free as frog-belch, and the mudlick of a river-terrace. Free as stars, blowing free around the sky, listing free to the wind's own sweet tilt. Here, there are no stars, no, and no night either.

◆

ANaRcHi
PELa
GO